Messy Hands

Written by Monica Hughes

Illustrated by Lisa Smith

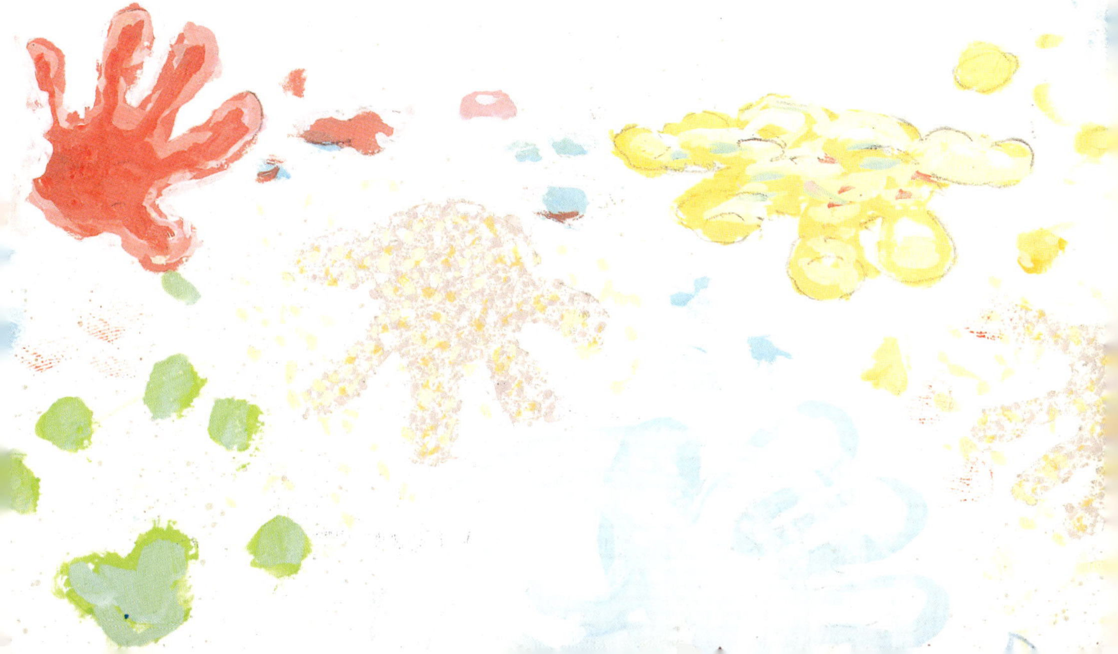

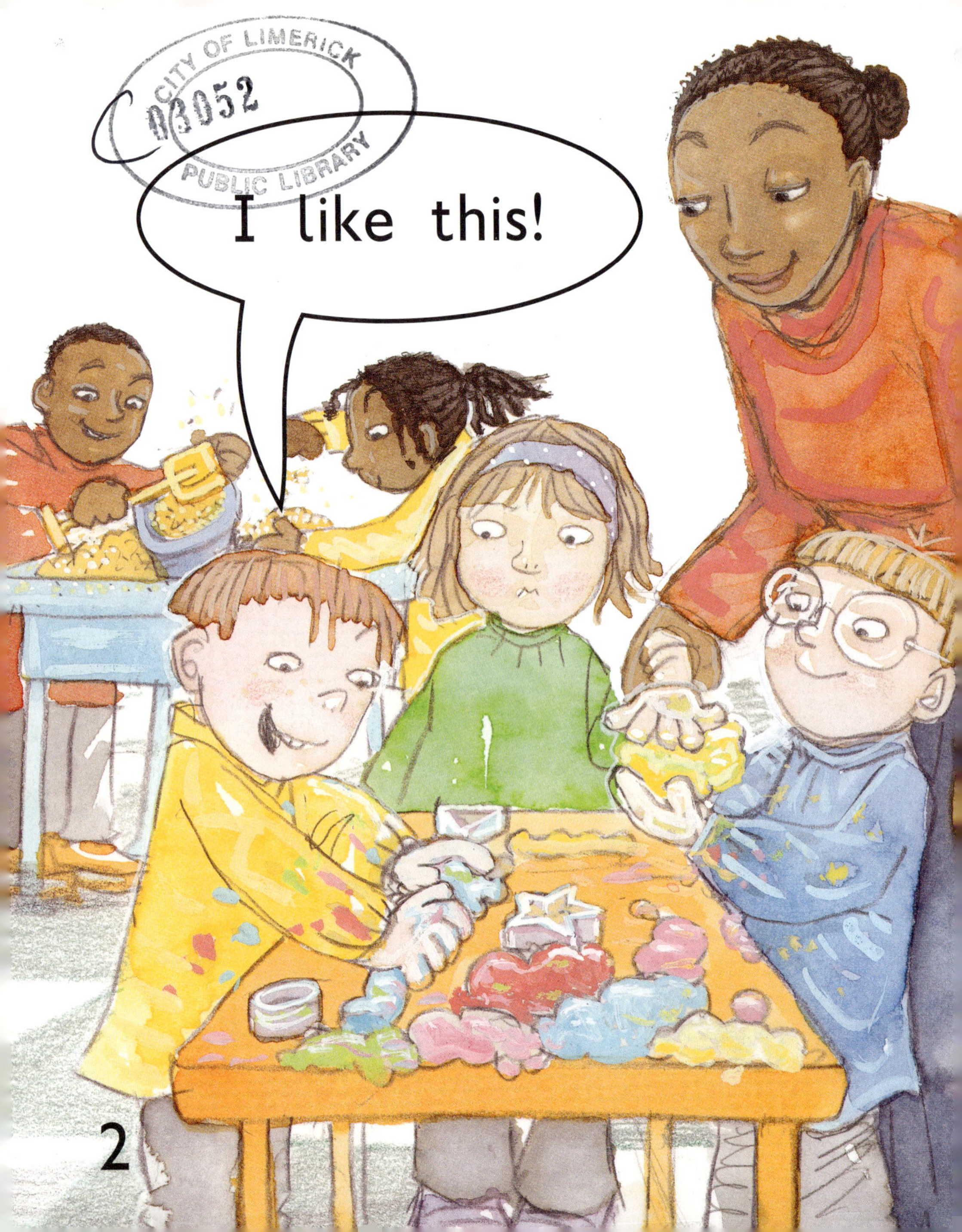
I like this!

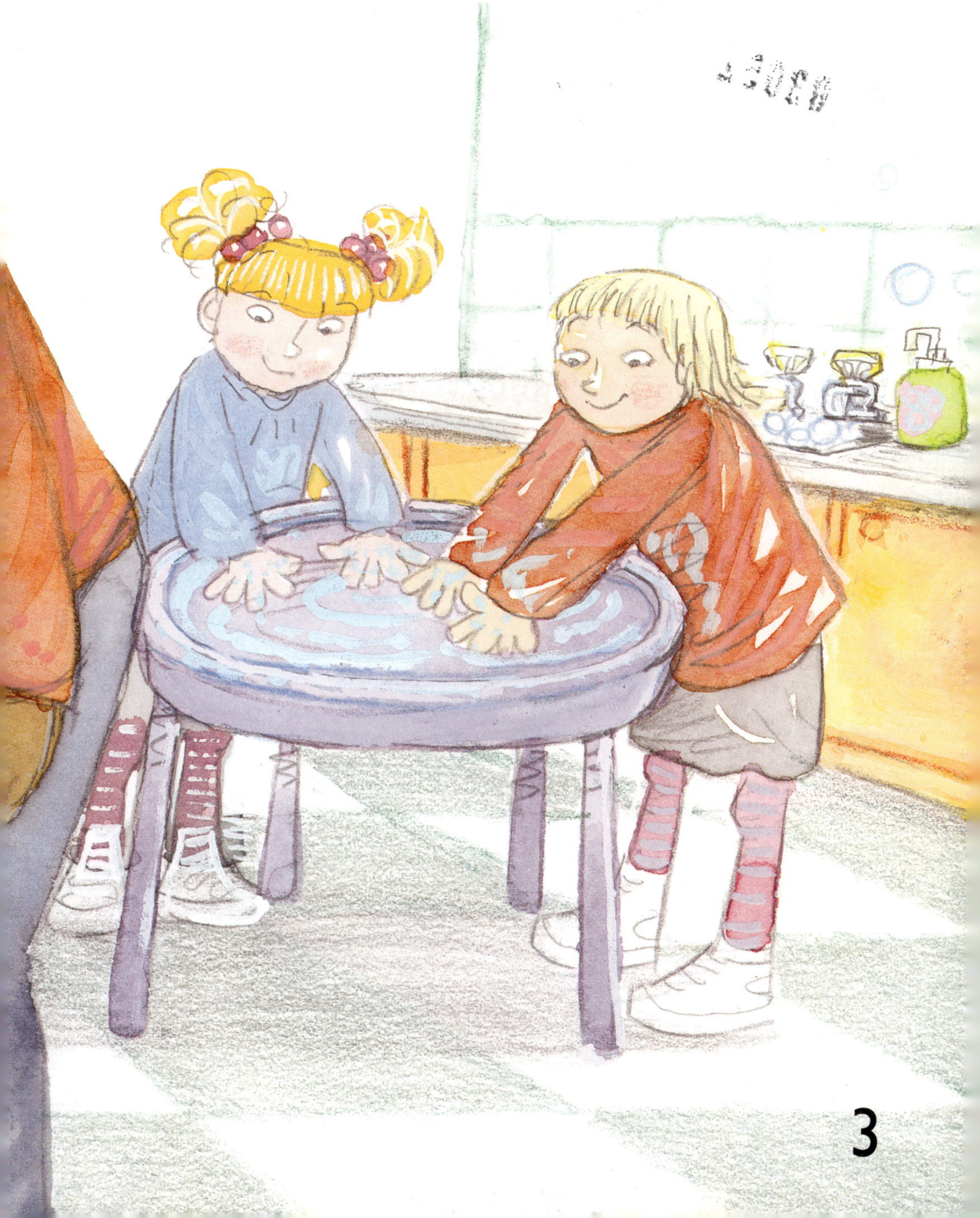

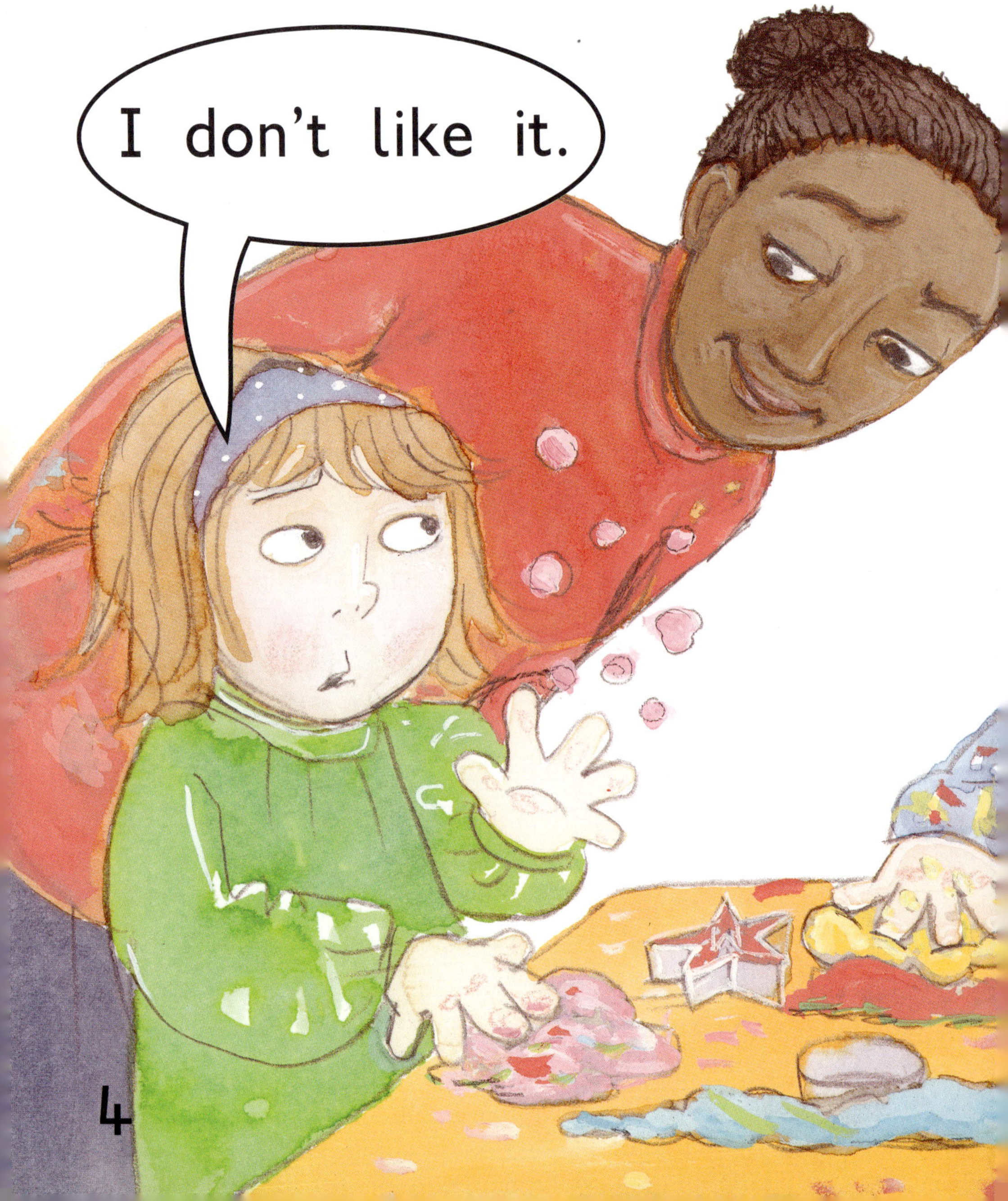
I don't like it.

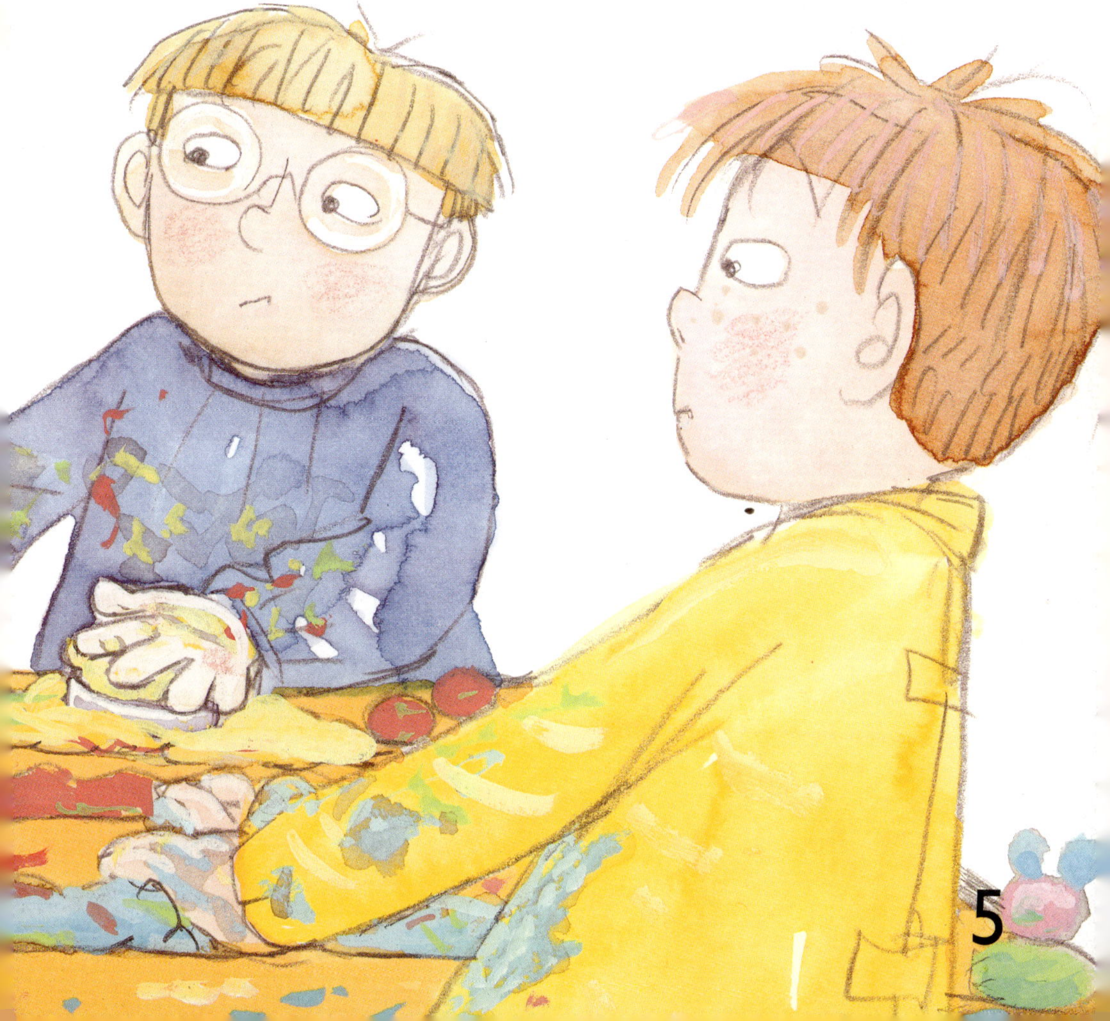

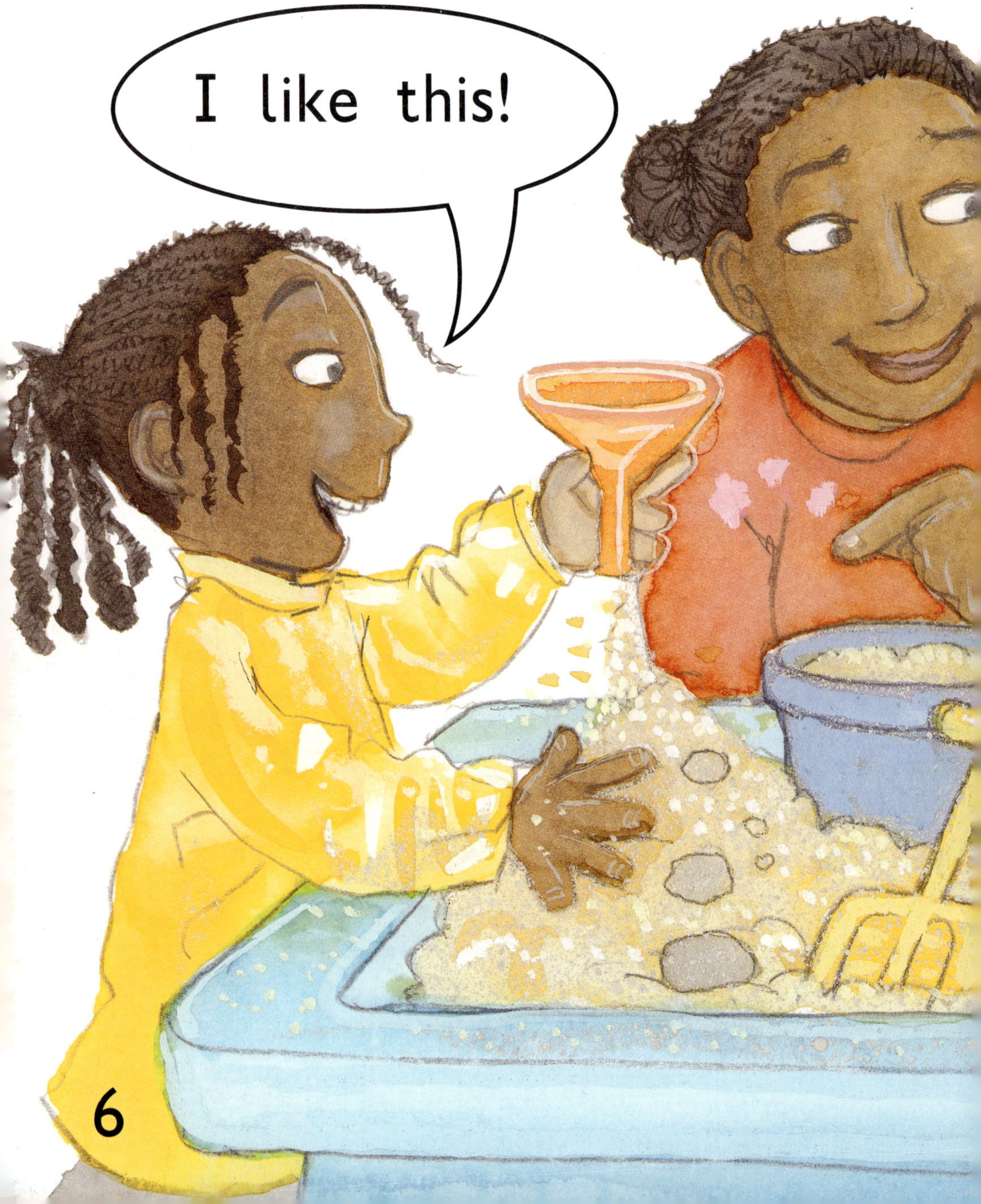
I like this!

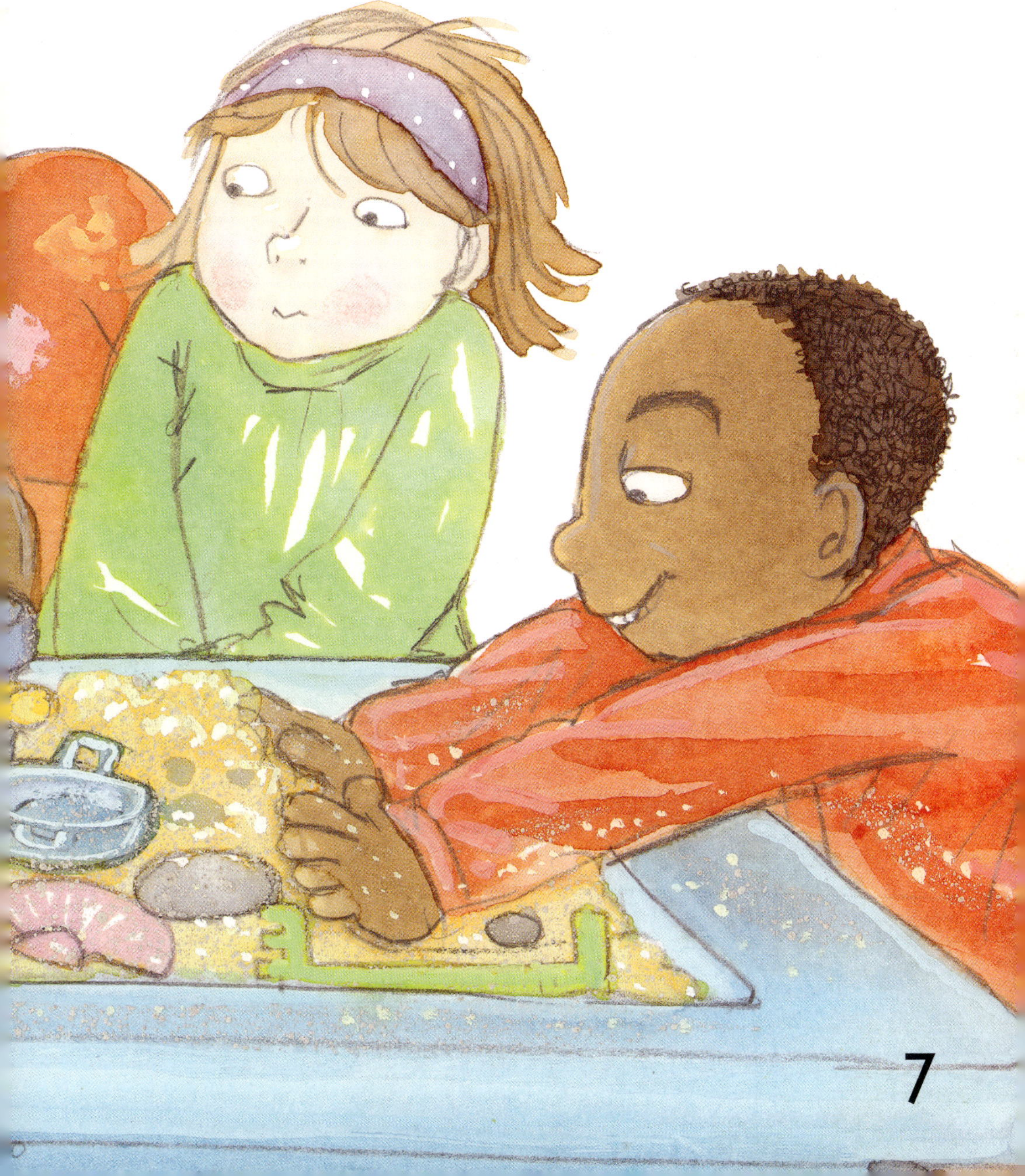

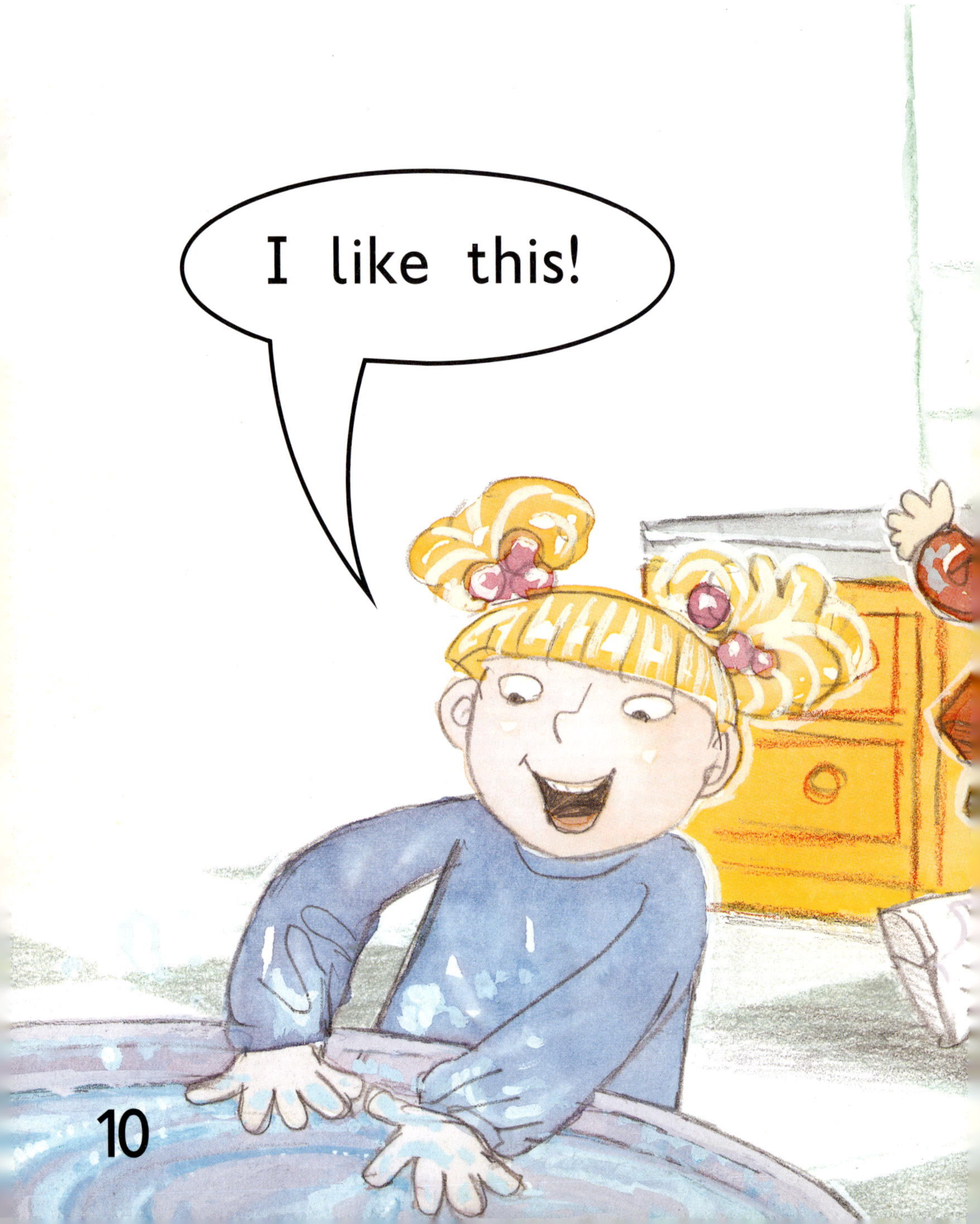
I like this!

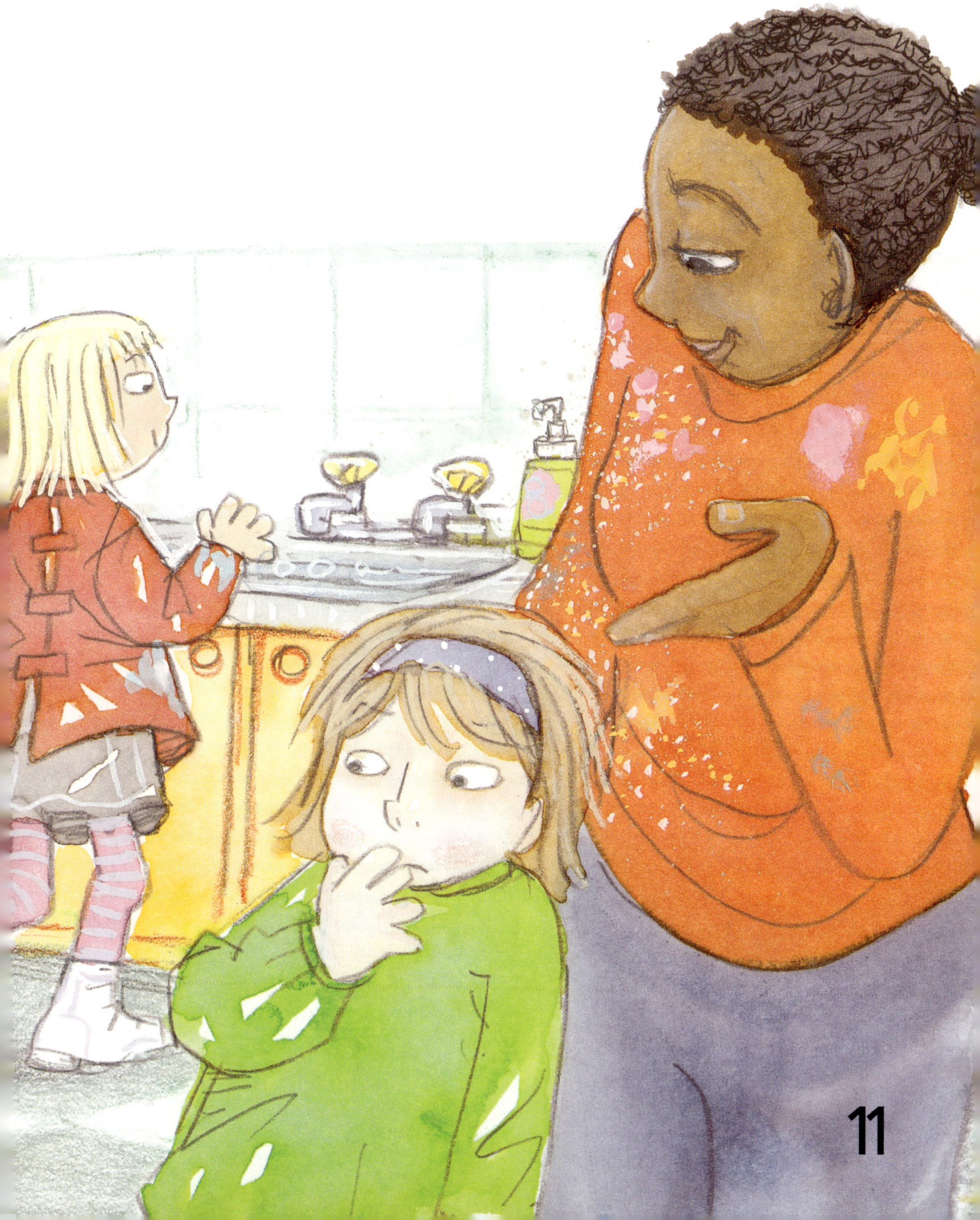

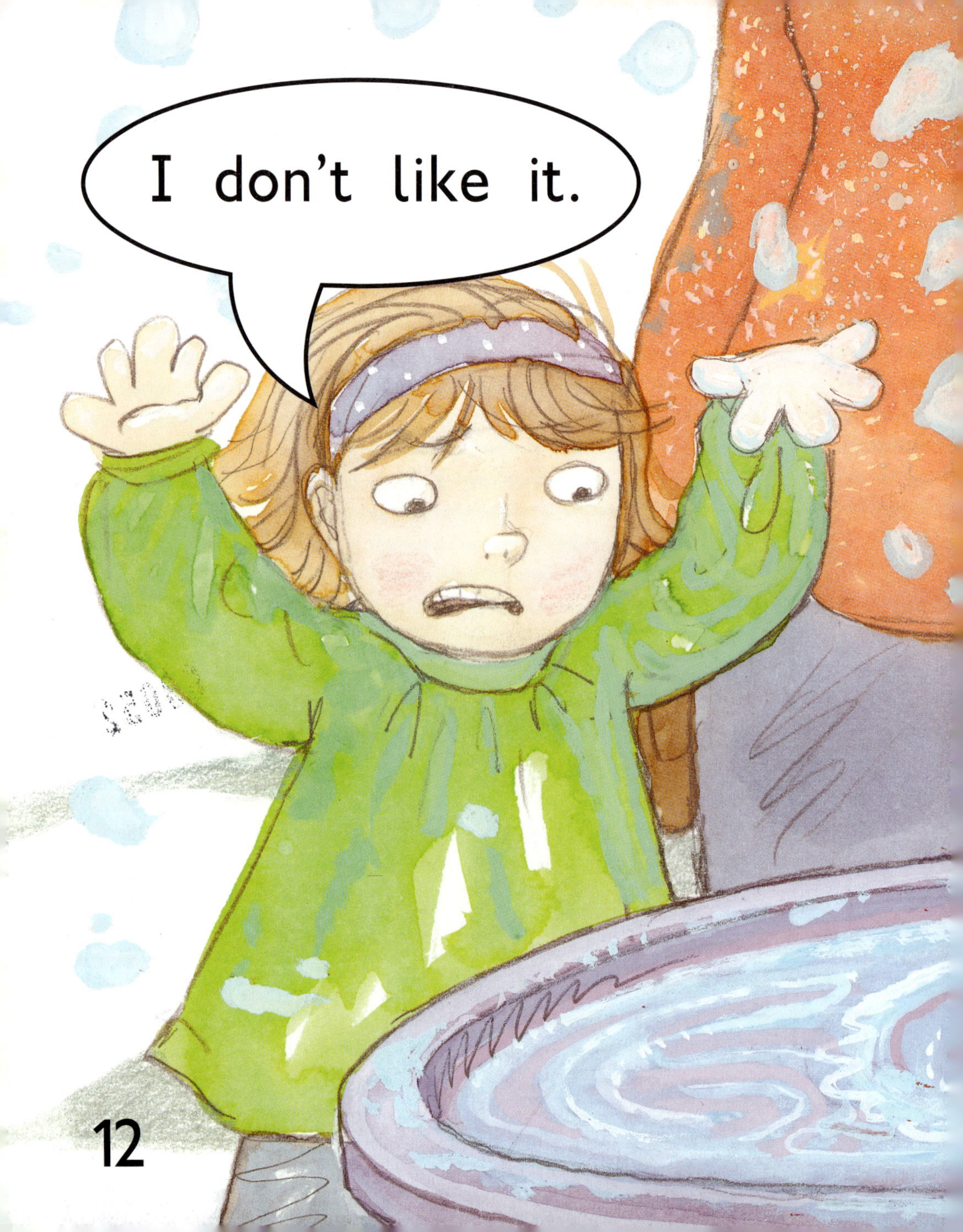
I don't like it.

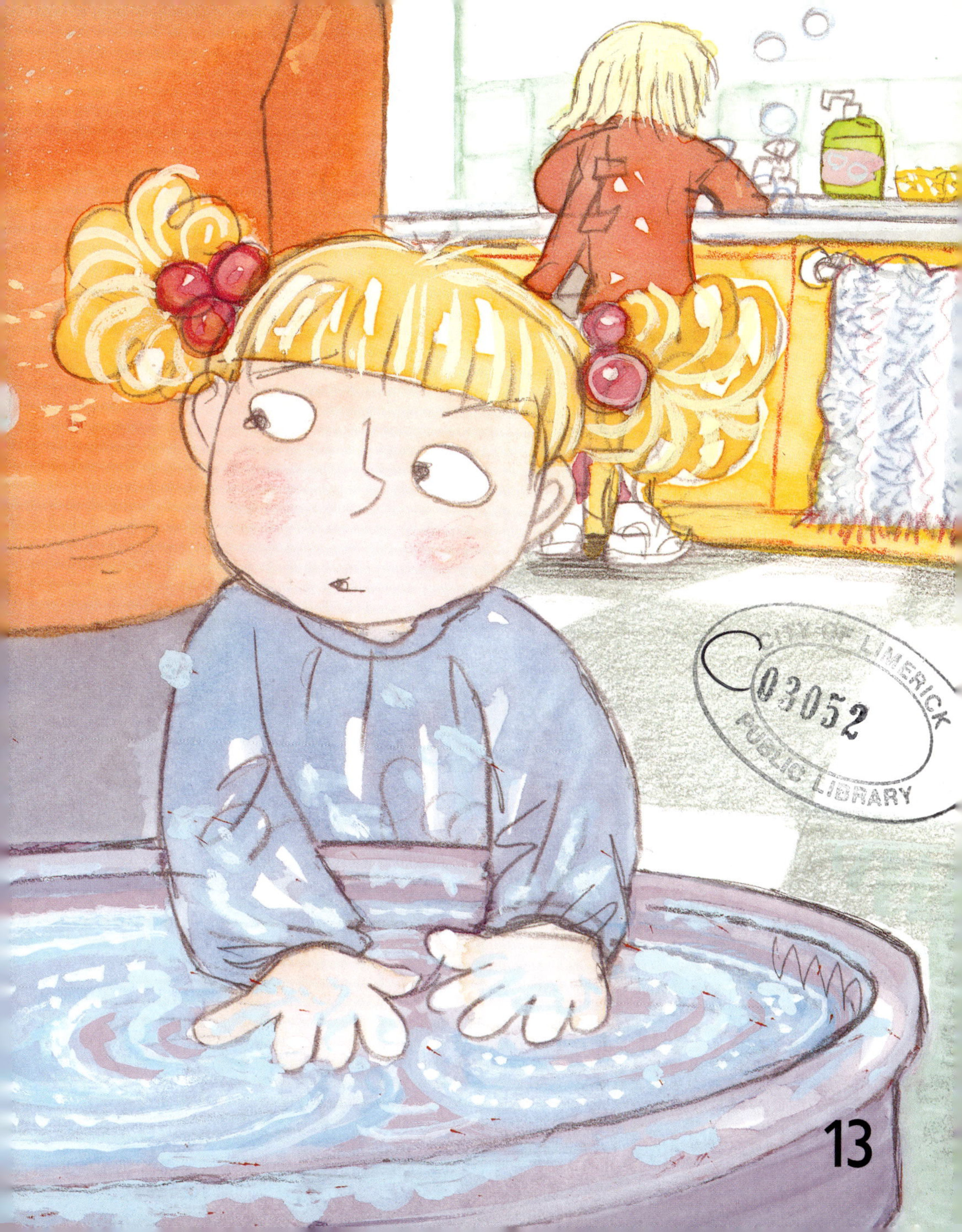

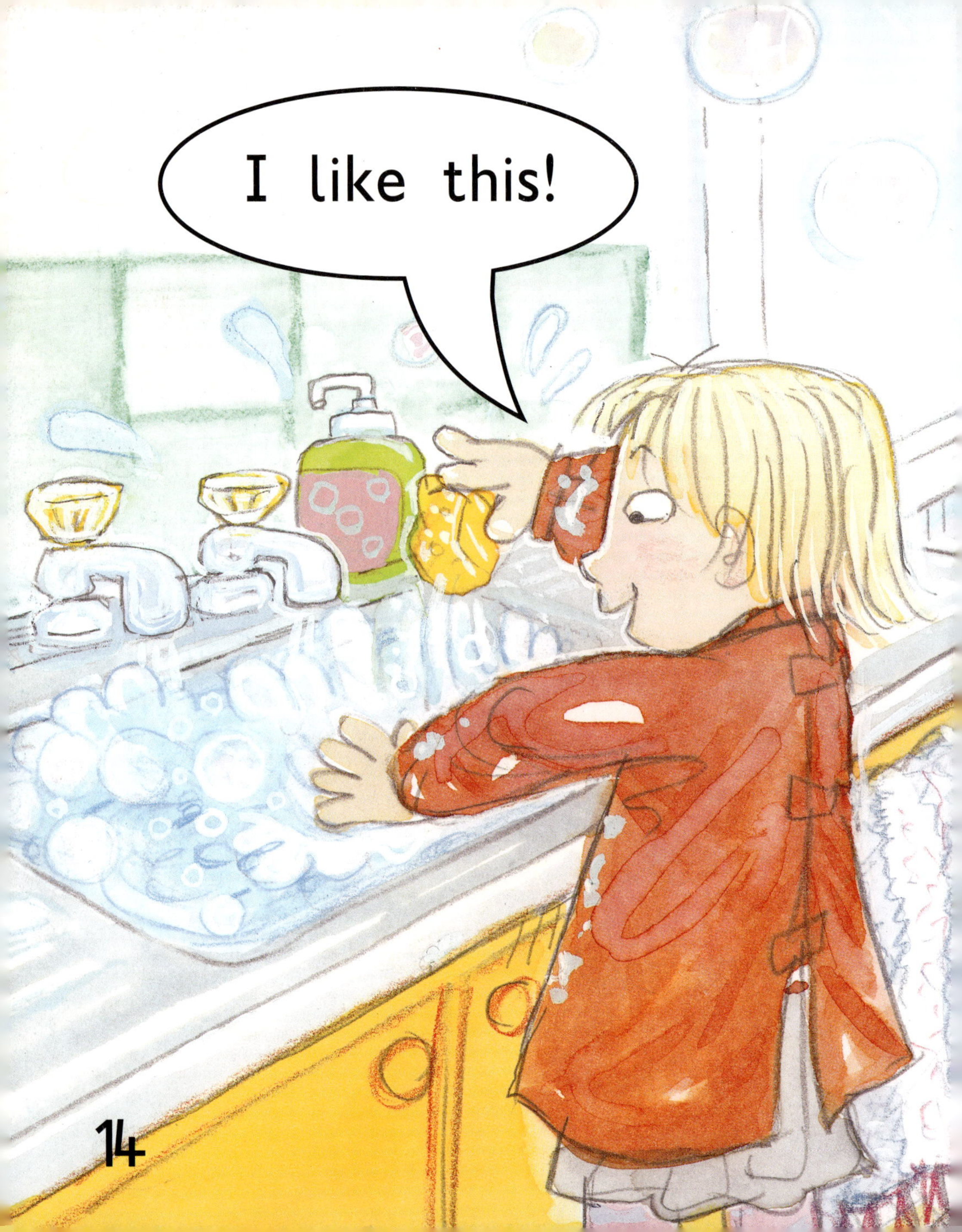
I like this!

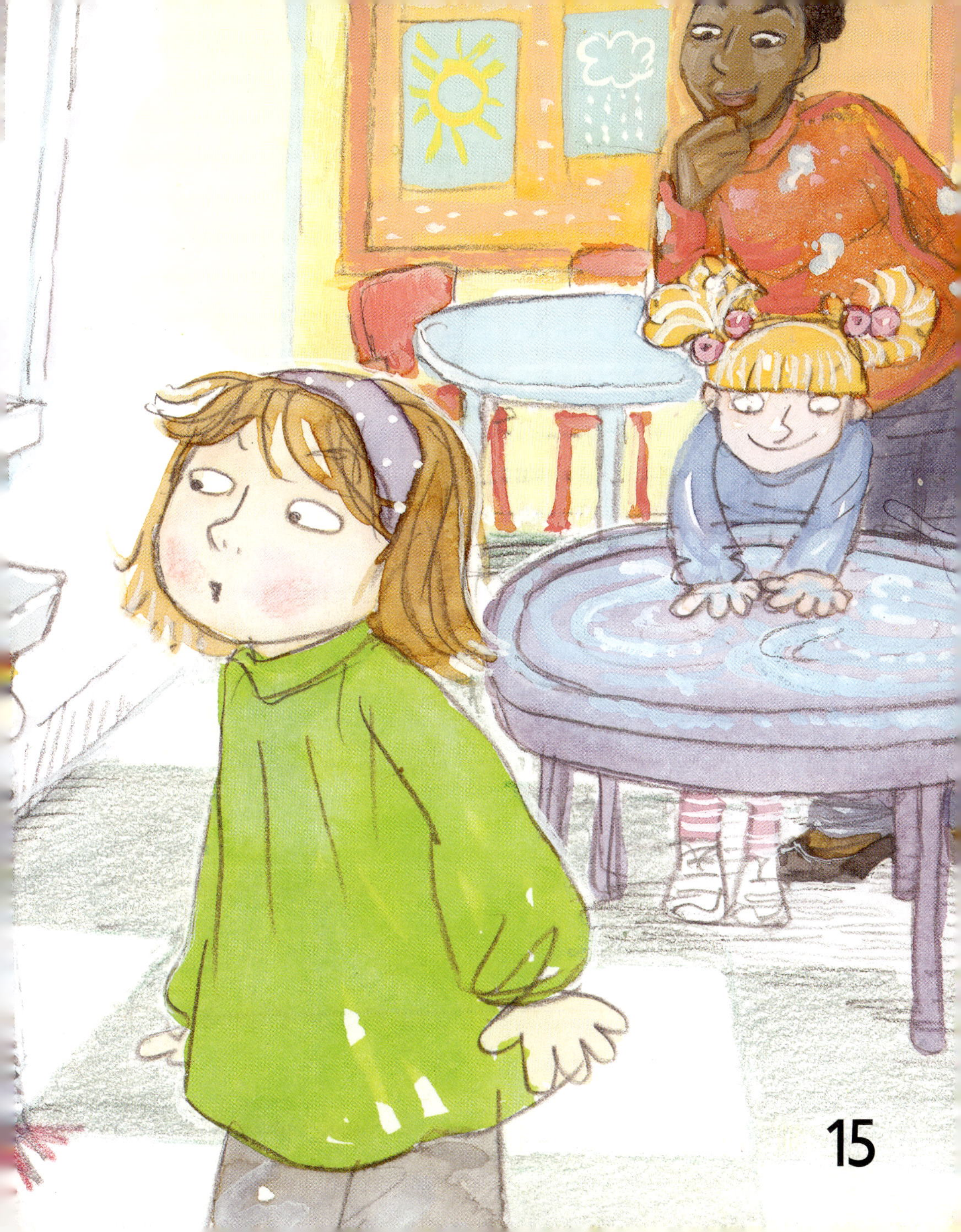

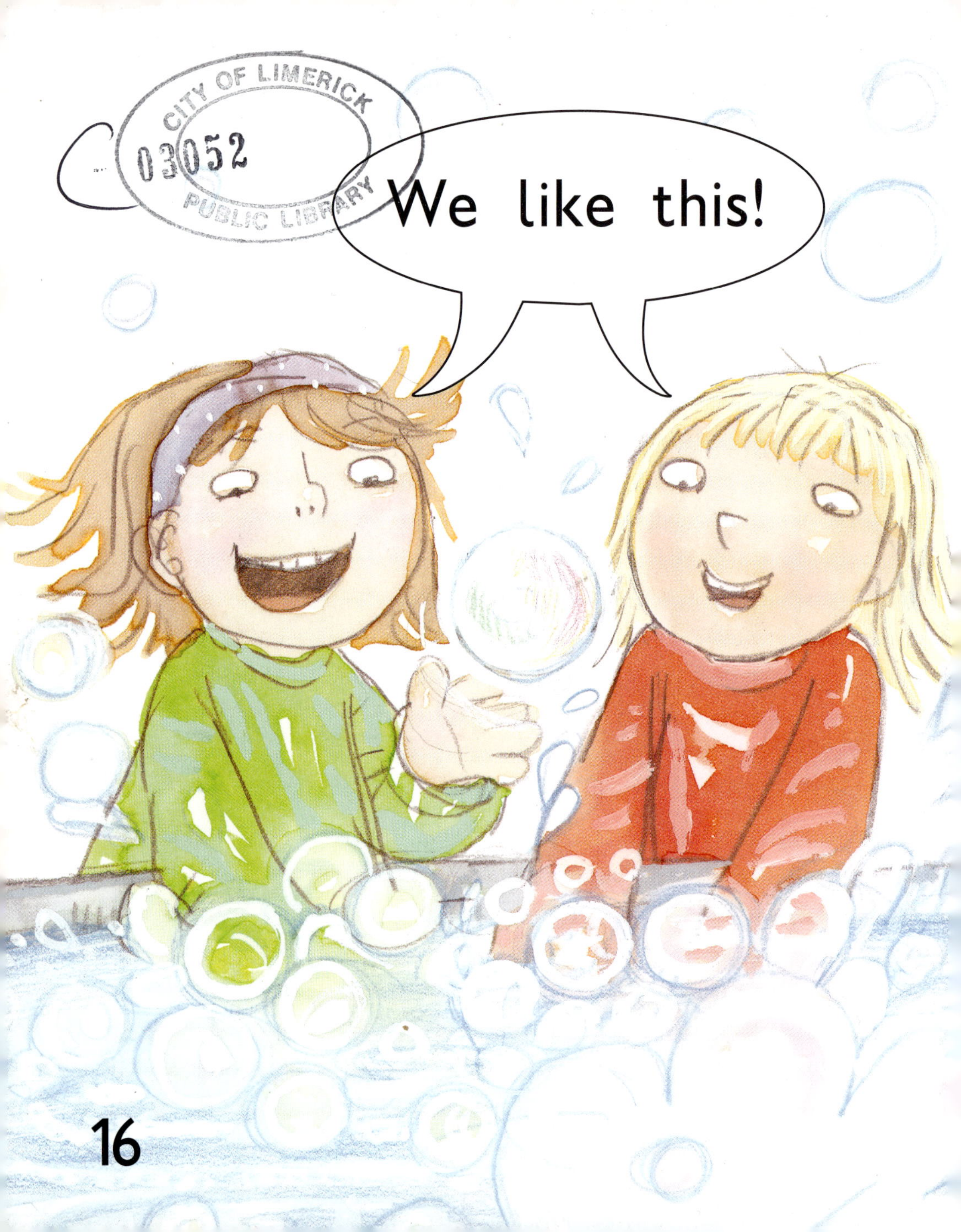
We like this!